WITHDRAWN

art
ACROSS the AGES

ANCIENT MEXICO

KELLY CAMPBELL HINSHAW

chronicle books · san francisco

Para mi madre hermosa, Rose

Permission to use the following photographs is gratefully acknowledged:

Front cover, title page, and page 7: © Michel Zabé/AZA; page 3, top row left: © Erich Lessing/Art Resource, NY; top row right: © Werner Forman/Art Resource, NY; second row left: © Werner Forman/Art Resource, NY; second row right: © Michel Zabé/AZA; bottom row left: © Werner Forman/Art Resource, NY; bottom row right: © Scala/Art Resource, NY; page 4: © Werner Forman/Art Resource, NY; page 5: © Werner Forman/Art Resource, NY; pages 8–9: © HIP/Art Resource, NY; page 10, top: © The Bodleian Library, University of Oxford, MS. Arch. Selden. A. 1, fol. 64r (detail); bottom: © Werner Forman/Art Resource, NY; page 11: © Werner Forman/Art Resource, NY; page 12: © Werner Forman/Art Resource, NY; page 13: © Tom Brakefield/Photodisc Green/Getty Images; page 14: © Werner Forman/Art Resource, NY; page 16: © Justin Kerr, K2888; page 19: © Doug Stern/National Geographic Image Collection; page 20: © Scala/Art Resource, NY; page 21: © David Lavender; page 22: © Werner Forman/Art Resource, NY; page 23: © Neil Beer/Photodisc Green/Getty Images; pages 24–25: © Erich Lessing/Art Resource, NY; page 26: © The Bodleian Library, University of Oxford, MS. Arch. Selden. A. 1, fol. 64r (detail); page 27: © Werner Forman/Art Resource, NY; page 28: © Werner Forman/Art Resource, NY; page 31: © Michel Zabé/AZA; page 32: photo © Schalkwijk/Art Resource, NY; artwork © 2007 Banco de México Diego Rivera & Frida Kahlo Museums Trust. Av. Cinco de Mayo No. 2, Col. Centro, Del. Cuauhtémoc 06059, México, D.F.

Book design by Kyle Spencer.
Typeset in Hermes and Bembo.
Manufactured in China.

Library of Congress Cataloging-in-Publication Data
Hinshaw, Kelly Campbell.
The art of ancient Mexico / Kelly Campbell Hinshaw.
p. cm. — (Art across the ages)
ISBN-13: 978-0-8118-5671-3 (pbk.)
ISBN-10: 0-8118-5671-2 (pbk.)
ISBN-13: 978-0-8118-5670-6 (hardcover)
ISBN-10: 0-8118-5670-4 (hardcover)
1. Indian art—Mexico—Juvenile literature. 2. Indians of Mexico—Antiquities—Juvenile literature.
3. Mexico—Antiquities—Juvenile literature. I. Title. II. Series.
F1219.3.A7C284 2007
704.03'97—dc22
2006026385

Distributed in Canada by Raincoast Books
9050 Shaughnessy Street, Vancouver, British Columbia V6P 6E5

10 9 8 7 6 5 4 3 2 1

Chronicle Books LLC
680 Second Street, San Francisco, California 94107

www.chroniclekids.com

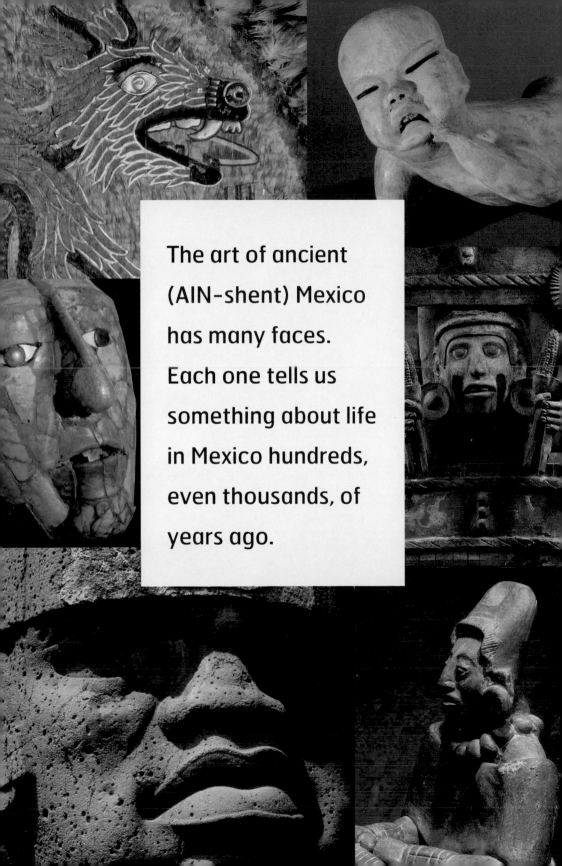

The art of ancient (AIN-shent) Mexico has many faces. Each one tells us something about life in Mexico hundreds, even thousands, of years ago.

Artists made all kinds of art in ancient
Mexico.

This clay sculpture is covered with shells.

A mighty wind god looks
out of a coyote's mouth.

Artists used materials from the earth like clay, stone, and gold.

This gold charm shows an ancient Mexican sun god.

Ancient Mexicans made art to honor their gods and goddesses.

This is a clay sculpture of a corn goddess. She wears a large headdress with flowers. People asked her to make the corn grow so there would be plenty of food.

Long ago she was painted bright red, yellow, and blue.
Can you still see some of the paint?

Ancient Mexicans also made art that showed people doing everyday things.

In this group sculpture, a mother and child listen to a drummer play music.

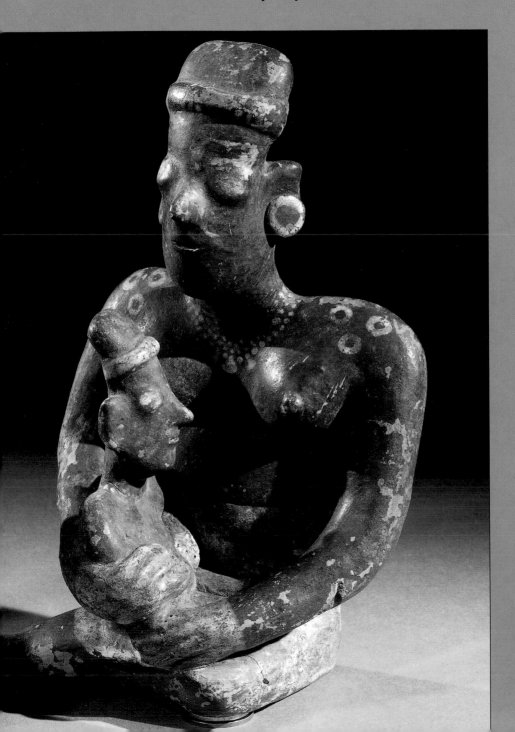

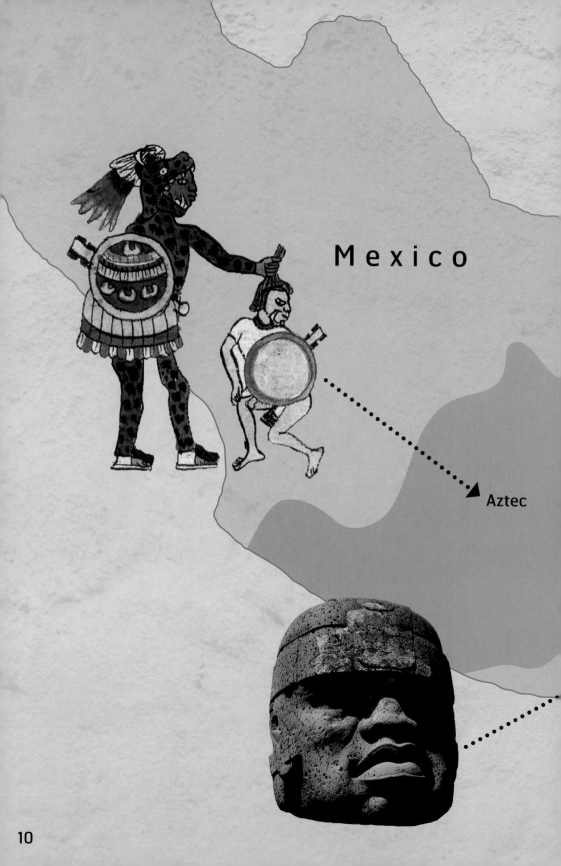

Mexico

Aztec

Over time, many groups of people lived in Mexico.

Three of the most powerful were

the Olmecs (OHL-meks),

the Maya (MY-ah),

and the Aztecs (AZ-teks).

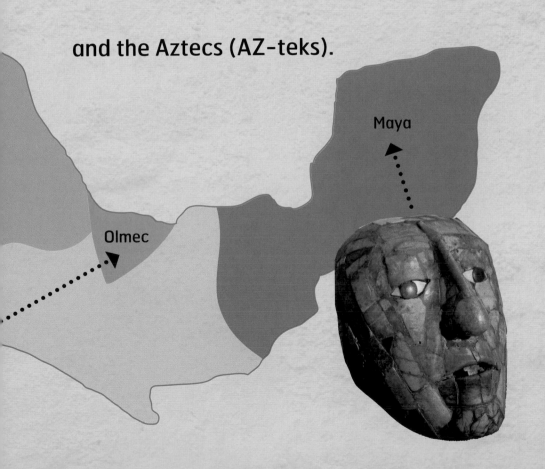

Maya

Olmec

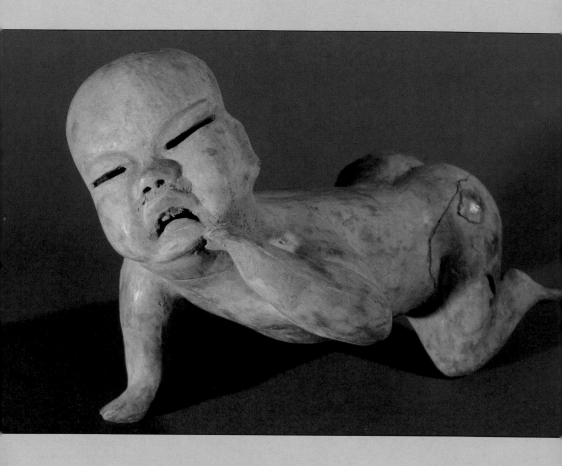

The Olmec people were the first to make art
in Mexico.

This sculpture of a baby was made of clay.

It is almost 3,000 years old!

The baby's face, like many faces in Olmec art, looks part jaguar.

The Olmecs loved and feared this strong jungle animal.

This giant head was carved from one large rock.
Was this a sculpture of an Olmec leader?
We don't know.
Four of these large heads stood in an ancient city near the ocean.

Do you think his face looks angry or proud?

The Maya people came after the Olmecs.

The Maya studied numbers and the stars.

They were also amazing artists.

This is a picture carved into stone.

The Maya god of war is coming out of a snake's mouth.

A queen holds a gift for the god.

This bright wall painting of Maya kings is over 1,000 years old.

The kings' heads are facing sideways. This shows off their slanted foreheads. The Maya thought slanted foreheads were beautiful.

The kings wear royal headdresses, capes, and jewelry.

Maya artists made small sculptures of people at work.
The woman in this clay sculpture sits at a loom.
She is weaving fabric.

The Maya still weave fabric today.
The woven cloth above is decorated with
jungle birds and flowers.

Jade was the Maya's favorite stone. Its blue-green color reminded them of water.

Small pieces of jade were fit together to make this mosaic (mo-ZAY-ik) mask. The eyes are made from shells.

A king wearing this jade mask was buried under the pyramid (PEER-a-mid) below.

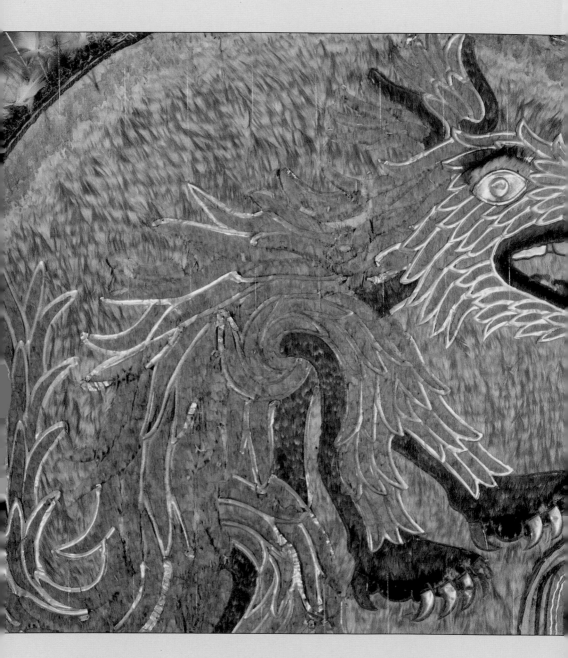

The monster—which might be a coyote—is outlined in gold.

The Aztecs were the last
rulers in ancient Mexico.
This Aztec shield was made
500 years ago.
It is decorated with hundreds
of feathers.
The Aztecs traded jewelry and
woven cloth for bird feathers.

The Aztecs were brave warriors.
The best fighters wore jaguar or eagle
costumes in battle.

This picture of a jaguar fighter and his prisoner is from an
Aztec book.

The folding book below is called a "codex." The story on each page was written in picture words.

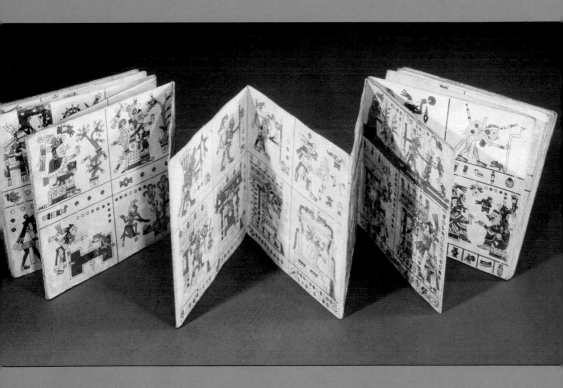

The Aztecs made paper from tree bark or animal skins.

This huge sculpture was found buried underground in Mexico City.
It is a stone carving of the Aztec earth goddess.

Her head is two rattlesnakes.

A skull is on her belt.

More snakes crawl over her skirt.

Aztec art can be scary!

A crouching monkey holds its tail on this Aztec pot.

It is made of black rock that came from a volcano.

Great skill was needed to carve the monkey.

Lots of polishing made it shine.

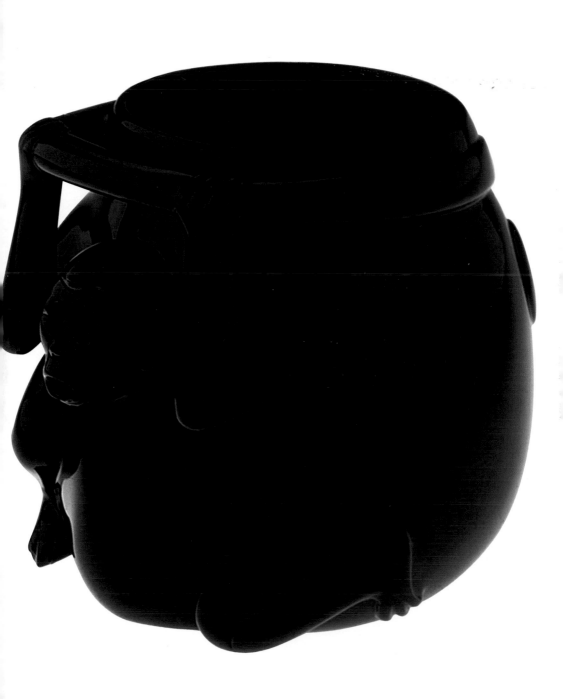

Without these works of art, we would know very little about the people of ancient Mexico and their world.

Today many Mexican artists are still inspired by the past.

In 1945 Diego Rivera painted this mural of an ancient Aztec market.